For Timothy and the North
Hampshire Hospital
Special Care Baby Unit
~ *J.S.*

For Emily Anna
~ *J.C.*

This edition produced 2005 for
BOOKS ARE FUN LTD
1680 Hwy 1 North, Fairfield, Iowa, IA 52556
by LITTLE TIGER PRESS
An imprint of Magi Publications
1 The Coda Centre, 189 Munster Road, London SW6 6AW
www.littletigerpress.com

Originally published in Great Britain 1997
by Little Tiger Press, London

Text copyright © Julie Sykes 1997
Illustrations copyright © Jane Chapman 1997

DORA'S EGGS

by *Julie* Sykes

illustrated by Jane Chapman

LITTLE TIGER PRESS

Dora was sitting on a nest of eggs.
They were shiny brown and smooth
to touch.
"These are my very first eggs,"
clucked Dora proudly. "I must
get all my friends to come
and admire them."

Dora climbed out of the henhouse and
into the farmyard.
"Who shall I visit first?" she wondered.
"I know! I'll go and find Debbie Duck."

Dora hopped over the fence and across the field until she reached the pond.
"Hello, Debbie," she called. "Would you like to come and see my eggs?"
"I can't come now," quacked Debbie. "I'm teaching my babies to swim."

Dora stood watching the ducklings
splashing around and learning to paddle.
Somehow she felt a bit less excited.
"My eggs are nice," she thought.
"But those fluffy ducklings are
much nicer."

Dora was just a little sad as she trotted
over to the sty to visit Penny Pig.
"Hello, Penny," she clucked. "Would you
like to come and see my eggs?"
But Penny didn't hear. She was having
too much fun tumbling around with her
wriggly piglets.

Dora gave a little sigh.
"My eggs are nice," she thought. "But
those wriggly piglets are much nicer."

Dora gave another little sigh as she climbed the hill to find Sally Sheep. "Would you like to come and see my eggs?" she asked Sally.
"Not today," bleated Sally. "I'm too busy keeping an eye on my lambs."

Dora looked at the lambs
frolicking in the field.
She felt rather glum.
"My eggs are nice," she
thought. "But those playful
lambs are much nicer."

Very sadly, Dora walked back to the farmyard.
On her way she bumped into Daisy Dog.
"Hello, Daisy," clucked Dora. "Would you like
to come and see my eggs?"
"Sorry, Dora," barked Daisy, wagging her tail.
"I can't come now. I'm taking my puppies
for a walk."

Dora was beginning to feel
quite miserable.
"My eggs are nice," she thought.
"But those cute puppies out
for a walk are much nicer."

In the farmyard Dora stopped
at the cow shed. She wished
she felt happier—perhaps
Clarissa the Cow would cheer
her up.

"Would you like to see my
eggs?" she called.

"Shhh," mooed Clarissa softly, nodding at the straw.
Snuggled up by her feet was a newborn calf, fast asleep.
Dora wanted to cry.
"My eggs are nice," she whispered. "But that
little calf all snuggled up is much nicer."

Dora walked back across the yard in the sunlight
and climbed into the henhouse. Her eggs were just as
she had left them, smooth and brown and very still.
"My eggs are nice," sighed Dora, fluffing out her
feathers. "But everyone else's babies are *much* nicer."

Very sadly, Dora settled
herself down onto
her nest . . .

CRACK!

Dora jumped up in surprise.

"Oh no!" cried Dora. "I've broken them!"
Tears began to roll down her face.
They splashed onto the nest and over
the cracked eggs. As each tear fell,
the cracks grew wider and wider until
suddenly . . .

. . . up popped a fluffy head,
then another, and another.

Soon the nest was full of
tiny chicks.
"Cheep, cheep," the chicks
peeped. "Cheep, cheep."
Dora stopped crying and
stared at her babies.

It didn't matter that the eggs were broken.
The new chicks were everything Dora had
ever wanted!
Proudly she strutted out into the farmyard,
and one by one the chicks followed after her.
All the animals stopped and looked.

"Why, Dora!" quacked Debbie.
"They're as fluffy as my ducklings!"
"And wriggly like my piglets,"
oinked Penny.
"They're as playful as my lambs,"
baaed Sally.
"And you can take them for walks—
just like my puppies," barked Daisy.
"But best of all," mooed Clarissa,
"your chicks can snuggle up to you,
like my calf snuggles up to me."
"Cluck," said Dora happily, agreeing
with her friends. "My eggs were
nice, but my chicks are much,
much nicer!"

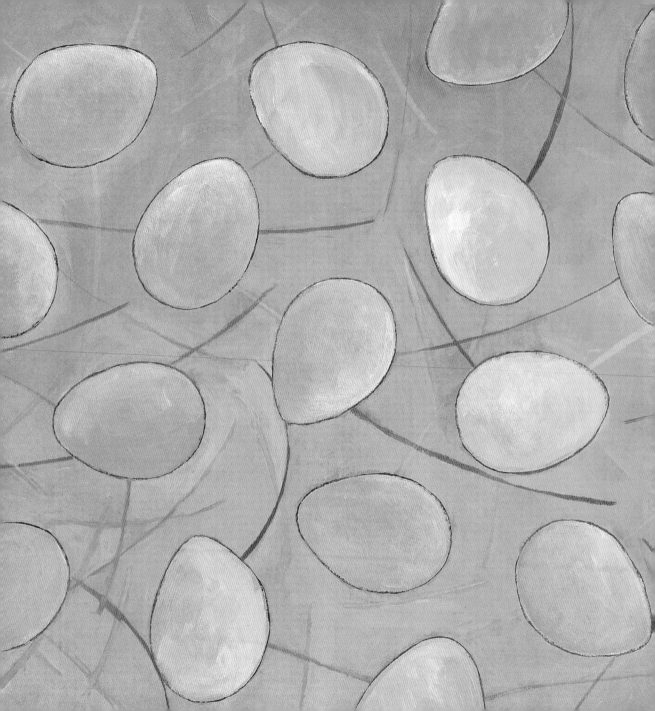